Judy West

The Christmas Owls

Illustrated by Gerda Westerink

Floris Books

Owl Soft and Owl Feather lived together at the top of a bell tower, inside the village church. It was a very cold December night.

"Let's snuggle closer," said Owl Soft to his friend. "It's so cold up here. I hope the children will come and light some candles. That always makes us feel warmer."

The next day was the first Sunday of December. That evening, children and their parents came to a service in the church. Owl Soft and Owl Feather watched them light the candles.

"Mmm, that's better," said Owl Soft to Owl Feather. "It's warm now. Look at all those candles."

As the people sang, one little boy looked up. He whispered to his mother. She looked and saw Owl Soft and Owl Feather nestling on their perch.

A few days later, Owl Soft and Owl Feather saw some men coming into the church with pieces of wood, hammers and nails.

"What's going on, Feather?" asked Owl Soft. "What are they making?"

"It looks like a kind of house," said Owl Feather as the men put the pieces of wood together. They flew down to a lower perch for a better look.

"What is it for, Feather?"

"I don't know, Soft," said Feather. "We'll have to wait and see."

The next day more men and women brought in bales of hay and straw. They spread the hay all over the floor of the little house. The owls watched.

"But this is a church," said Owl Soft. "What are they doing? Do you think they've brought some food for us — some fieldmice hidden in the straw and hay, perhaps?"

Owl Feather just grunted.

Next the men put a manger in the middle of the little house and filled it with hay.

"What's that?" asked Soft.

"It's a manger," said Feather, "where horses and cows have their hay to eat."

"It looks like a baby's cradle," said Soft.

"Tonight we'll fly down and look at it." said Feather.

That night they swooped down over the manger.

"No sign of anything to eat there, Soft," said Feather beating his wings. "They've made a sort of stable inside the church. I don't know what it's all about," declared Owl Feather.

The next day the same men brought in some animals and some people.

"But they're not moving," said Soft. "What's the matter with them?"

"They aren't real animals, Soft, and they aren't real people!" said Owl Feather.

"One of them is dressed like a shepherd. He's gazing at the manger," said Owl Soft.

"We'll fly down again tonight and have another look," Feather decided.

Owl Soft and Owl Feather flew down that night and
settled in the stable.

"I was right," said Owl Feather, preening himself. "The people aren't real. That shepherd is made of wood. So is that sheep! And this cow!"

"So what's it all about, Feather?" asked Soft.

"I don't know," said Owl Feather, shaking his head. "Let's go and hunt for some church mice."

The next day more people came into the church. They brought in holly, fir, ivy, and a very big tree.

"Feather," said Owl Soft, "I think something special is happening down there."

"I wish they'd leave us alone," said Owl Feather. "We get no peace at all."

The owls watched as the people decorated the tree and put small lights on it. They put the holly, fir and ivy all around the church and on the pulpit.

Later that night it was cold and quiet.

"There's something in the manger now," said Owl Soft. "Shall we go down and have another look?"

"Good idea," said Owl Feather. "Ready?" The owls launched into the air.

"Oh no, we can't," said Owl Feather. "The people are coming in again."

"But it's nearly midnight!" said Soft.

"Yes, it's our time in the church," moaned Owl Feather. "And I want to hunt for mice."

Lots of people came into the church although
it was nearly midnight. There were even small
children in the church.

They sang and lit candles just as if it were a
Sunday morning.

"Soft, I don't understand it," said Feather.
"Let's fly down anyway and see what's going on."

Owl Soft and Owl Feather flew down into the church. They swooped low over the people's heads and they flew low over the manger.

The people looked up from their singing, amazed.

"It's the owls!" cried out the little boy.

"Sh!" whispered his mother, frowning at him.

"The angel from the Lord came down," they sang, as the owls flew overhead yet again.

The singing finished. Owl Soft and Owl Feather fluttered down and sat above the manger, beside the angels. They looked down and saw that now there was a baby, lying in a manger.

"Look at the owls!" murmered the little boy. "They're just like the angels."

"Maybe, in a way they *are* angels," whispered his mother. "They watched from on high and now they've come down to share something special. It's almost as if they understand what it's all about."

"They do understand," said the little boy. "I'm sure they do."

"Feather," said Owl Soft later, when all the people had gone and they were back up on their perch. "Do you know what?"

"*What*, Soft?" said Owl Feather trying to get to sleep at last.

"The baby in the manger was real."

"No," said Owl Feather, sighing loudly, "the animals weren't real and the people weren't real either."

"But, Feather, the *baby*," insisted Owl Soft. "It was a special baby. The people were singing about him. He's called Baby Jesus. He *is* real."

"Goodnight, Soft," said Owl Feather. "Let's try to get some sleep."

"Good night, Feather," said Owl Soft. "Merry Christmas."